The Runaway Christmas Bride

©2024 by Cassie McCall

D1733529

Contents

Chapter 1

"Ella! I need to see you in the library for a minute!" Mr. Price's deep voice boomed up the stairs of their Boston home.

Ella frowned in the mirror. She'd almost finished with her hair, and she was running out of time before she was scheduled to have a nice tea with Bertie. Her friend had been so busy with wedding preparations that they'd hardly had any time to get together, and Ella knew that if she missed this appointment she might never get another one. After all, Bertie was bound to have even less time on her hands once she was married. "I'll be down in a moment!"

Putting the last pin in place and checking the mirror one last time for any stray hairs, Ella hurried down the stairs. She smiled a little to herself as her skirt flew around her, remembering how her governess used to get onto her for rushing through the house. She claimed it wasn't ladylike and didn't suit a young woman of her means and social status. Ella knew she was right, but one couldn't be perfect all the time.

"Yes?" she asked breathlessly as she stepped into the library. It doubled as her father's office, and his large oak desk was parked in front of massive bookshelves that were loaded with books. Some families had libraries simply to showcase how many books they could buy, but Ella knew her father had read every single volume in here.

"Are you in a hurry?" he asked, looking up from the ledgers spread out before him.

Mr. Price had always been more tolerant than either her governess or her mother. Ella smiled. "I am. I'm having tea with Bertie."

"Ah, yes. I believe you said something about that at dinner last night. Is she excited about her upcoming nuptials?" He picked up a pen and made a note.

"Oh, yes. She has everything planned out to a tee, and she is thrilled to become Mrs. John Henderson. I'm sure it's going to be the wedding of the year." In fact, she knew that Bertie had done everything possible to ensure that it was. It would be an elite affair with all of society's best, and not a cent was being spared.

Mr. Price bobbed his head, which had started going gray in recent years. "Wonderful, splendid. Your mother and I got our invitation in the mail, and we'll be happy to attend. It turns out, though, that Bertie isn't the only one with a big event coming up."

"Oh?" Ella glanced at the clock, trying not to show her impatience. Normally, she'd love to chat with her father about things like Bertie's wedding, but not right now.

"No, no. There's going to be another wedding coming up, and one that I think will be just as much of a to-do as Bertie's. In fact, it might even be bigger."

"Really?" Ella tipped her head as she tried to think. "Did Joshua Mills finally propose to Evie Harris? Rumor has it that he's been interested in her for quite some time, but he hasn't quite gotten up the gumption to ask for her hand."

Her father grinned. "No, this is even better than that! Ella, I've made all of the arrangements myself. This fall, you'll be marrying Sheldon Jones."

The excitement she'd felt for her tea with Bertie suddenly drained straight out of her body along with all of her strength. She stepped back into the leather armchair that she knew was waiting right behind her, plopping down—in a rather unladylike fashion—onto the cushion before she fell to the floor.

Mr. Price laughed. "I see the good news has completely stunned you! I thought you might be pleased, especially knowing what a tidy fortune Sheldon is expected to inherit someday."

"I…I…" Ella searched for the right words to tell him. She didn't *want* to marry Sheldon Jones! Any protest on her part would have to be carefully worded, however. Her father was a kind and generous man, as long as things were going his way. He wouldn't take it well if she balked. "Does mother know?" she managed to ask.

"Oh, yes. In fact, she went rushing straight off to her seamstress to order new dresses for the both of you so that you can look your best when she invites everyone over for dinner and makes the official announcement."

"My goodness." Not only was this happening, but it was happening without her. Ella had never been asked for her opinion, not for the choice of dress or even the groom.

"I don't like to indulge her *too* much, since we both know your mother could spend a small fortune on clothing in the matter of an afternoon, but I can certainly understand in this case. After all, it's not every day that the children of the two biggest shipping magnates in the area get married!"

She nodded. The statement was true, but she certainly didn't like it.

"This will be just wonderful, Ella. It'll be the culmination of many years' worth of work. This will create such a solid company that it will guarantee a profitable income for generations to come. You'll never have to worry about a thing!" He slapped the edge of his desk in glee, clearly quite proud of himself.

There had to be some way out of this. "What does Sheldon think of the match?"

"Oh, you don't need to be concerned, my dear. I met with both he and his father this morning, and so he's been involved right from the start. He finds it a most advantageous union, and he knows that you'll be an asset to his household."

Ella lowered her lashes, staring down at the patterned carpet beneath her feet and wishing she could hide under it. Her insides were in turmoil, and she could sit here no longer. "Thank you for the good news, Father. I really must be getting to Bertie's now."

"Can't wait to tell her, can you? Mind you, my dear, she might be a little steamed when she finds that you've outdone her. Be gentle," he advised with a smile.

"I'll do that." A few minutes ago, Ella had been so concerned about getting to tea on time. Suddenly, there were far more important things in the world. She moved slowly from the library, holding herself back. Even once she was outside and had descended the steps, Ella knew she couldn't simply pick up her skirts and run. Someone would see, and there was no telling what sort of scandal might come of it. Ella Price, running down the sidewalk in the middle of the afternoon? She reached Bertie's house, but she hurried around the side to the back porch instead of entering through the front door.

"Oh, Ella! How nice to see you!" Bertie beamed when she saw her friend. "I do hope you didn't ruin your shoes on the grass. Thurman just cut it this morning."

"It doesn't matter." Ella collapsed into the chair across from her childhood friend. She waited until Bertie had shooed the maid away before she spoke. "Father has arranged a marriage between myself and Sheldon Jones."

Bertie's eyes widened. She adjusted the skirt of her dress and cleared her throat. "Manners dictate that I must congratulate you on your engagement, but Ella, Sheldon Jones?"

"I'm afraid so," Ella confirmed. "Father thinks it's a wonderful match, but that's only because he's looking at it with business connections and investments in mind. He's not thinking about love or happiness."

"I'm afraid most men don't," Bertie frowned. "I've been rather fortunate in that department."

"Yes, you have," Ella agreed. John Henderson was a true gentleman, and he genuinely cared for Bertie. Her friend had the perfect situation, but it was a rare one. "I don't know what to do, Bertie. I simply can't marry Sheldon Jones. I can hardly even stand to be in the same room with him!"

Bertie poured them each a cup of tea and passed the sugar. She frowned thoughtfully. "I don't suppose you have any other prospects, do you? Perhaps someone you'd actually tolerate whom your father would accept?"

"No. None." She'd never been very worried about her future, convinced that it would all work out as it went along. That was certainly what had happened for Bertie, but not for her. "Neither of my parents even asked what I thought, but Sheldon knows all about it."

Bertie's frown deepened. "That makes the problem even worse. It would be scandalous to call off the engagement."

Ella set her teacup down with a clink. "You're not suggesting that I actually go through with this, are you?"

Tipping her head and giving Ella a sympathetic look, Bertie nodded. "I don't see any way to back out of this. Though Sheldon Jones is not exactly a handsome man, and though he's an absolute bore, you can't deny that he's a very eligible bachelor in terms of his finances and his future."

"I don't care about that," Ella protested.

"But you have to," Bertie insisted. "You need someone to take care of you, and Sheldon can certainly do that."

Ella's mouth had gone dry. She knew that her friend was only trying to look out for her, but she felt betrayed. Everyone was going to force her to marry a man she didn't love, to tie her future to someone who had no other qualities than his money. Yes, money was important. She hadn't lived such a spoiled life as to not know that, but there had to be something more.

"Oh, Jenny forgot to put the lemon slices out. I'll just ring for her."

"Don't bother. I'll get them myself."
Ella stood up.

"But—" Bertie began.

"No, it's all right. I need a moment."
Ella stepped in through the back door and
went into the kitchen. The plate of lemon
slices was right there on the table. She fumed
as she picked it up. How could Bertie support
this terrible idea?

A newspaper lay just to the right. Ella
only glanced at it, but then she glanced back
again just before she walked away. *The
Matrimonial Times.* This wasn't a typical
newspaper. She turned through a few of the
pages, finding advertisements from men and
women seeking each other's company and
their hands in marriage. It was an odd notion,
and yet it intrigued her. If she was already

married, then she couldn't possibly be forced to marry Sheldon. If she moved out West, where many of the men listed seemed to be from, then she'd be free of her overbearing parents and all of their expectations. There was that added bonus that moving off to another state meant she wouldn't have to deal with the fallout of her broken engagement. Maybe there was a solution to her problem after all.

Chapter 2

"Did you have a nice trip into town today?"

"A productive one." Wade Monroe spooned another helping of mashed potatoes onto his plate. His mother was an excellent cook. "I had the horse reshod. The blacksmith wasn't as busy as he usually is, so I didn't have to wait long. Then I stopped at the bank, the general store, and the post office. It was all fairly normal."

"Did we have any mail?"

"There was a letter to you from your cousin Rose. I left it in my jacket, but I'll get it for you after supper." Wade drizzled dark brown gravy over his potatoes. Yes, he was very fortunate that his mother had decided to move in with him after his father died.

Rita Monroe lifted her nose slightly. "You know, Rose's son is going to be married next month."

"James? Well, good for him." Wade tried to pretend that this was a casual conversation, but he knew it was anything but. He had to give his mother some credit for finding a way to work marriage so naturally into their discussion, though he'd have much preferred to avoid it. "I heard he had moved out to California and had done well in construction. They need someone to build those boom towns, and I'll bet James is good at it. He's always had an eye for these things."

"And apparently he has an eye for finding himself a pretty young woman," Rita replied, not letting her son distract her from her favorite topic.

"Good for him." It was nice to have his mother here to run the household, and he couldn't deny how comforting it was to always have a hot meal waiting for him when he came in from a long day in the pastures. There were plenty of benefits to Rita Monroe's presence, but Wade paid for it almost every day with a lecture about being a bachelor.

"It's high time you did the same," his mother asserted. "You have a home and some land. You run a profitable business with this ranch. You're certainly handsome. There's no reason at all that you shouldn't have a wife."

She no doubt thought she could wear him down and convince him. The truth was that the more she talked about it, the less interest he had in walking down the aisle. "I don't need a wife."

"You do if I'm ever going to have grandchildren!" Rita snapped.

"Then there's the fact that I don't know any women I'd like to marry. In case you haven't noticed, Mother, there's not exactly an abundance of women out here. I can't just go into town, pick out a bride, and bring her home." If he was honest with himself, Wade had occasionally thought that it might be nice to have a wife. His mother wouldn't always be around, and he wouldn't mind having a few children. He wasn't getting any younger, but he had time.

"You don't even need to do that." Rita turned her head slightly to the side, a spark in her eye. "There's always Tess Ingram. I know she's got her eye on you."

"I think that's more of her mother's doing," Wade mumbled as he scraped the last of the mashed potatoes off his plate. "Ida Ingram likes to interfere just as much as you do."

"It's not interfering when the two of you are clearly meant to be together," Rita reasoned as she picked up their plates and carried them to the basin. "Ida and I have been friends for a long time. We know our children well, and we know what would be good for them. I don't see anything wrong with that."

"I don't love her, Mother."

"But you at least like her, and you'd come to love her in time." Rita rinsed and washed the plates before putting them on the drying rack. She toweled her hands off on her apron and then turned to check the oven. "The pie is done."

"I don't think I'm in the mood for pie. As a matter of fact, I think there are a few things I need to do in the barn before it gets dark." Wade scraped his chair back and stood up. He loved his mother, and he knew she had the best intentions, but there were only so many times that he could have the same conversation.

"Don't got out to the barn and pout. You always used to do that as a child, and nothing has changed. You can't just avoid your problems with work, Wade. It's not good for you," Rita pointed out.

Well, maybe she was right in a way, but she didn't understand how much easier it was for him to think when he went out to the barn alone, with nothing to listen to but the gentle whuff of a horse or the fluttering of the swallows that had made a nest up in the eaves. "I've just got some thinking to do."

"About marrying Tess?" she asked hopefully. "It really doesn't take any thought at all. I've seen her needlework, and she wouldn't have the least bit of trouble sewing or repairing almost anything in the house. She's also an excellent cook, but you already know that. You've sampled her creations several times when we've had dinner together or she's brought something to the church potluck. She's beautiful, too. And pleasant. Yes, she's really quite the catch."

He'd heard all of this before. None of it was inaccurate, really, but for Wade it just didn't add up to love. "Mother, please."

Rita put her fists on her hips, no longer trying to cajole him with sweet talk or his sweet tooth. "Well, you need to find a wife, and I don't see you marrying anyone else!"

A smile tugged at the corner of his mouth. He tried to stop it, but it was too late.

Rita had already seen it, and her eyes widened. "You can't have found some other woman! There aren't any in the area."

No, there certainly weren't. "Don't get your hopes up, Mother, not about Tess or anyone else. I'll be in the barn." He stepped past her and escaped down the short path. The night air was getting cooler, and he heard the wrinkle of paper as he pulled his jacket around him. Wade slipped into the barn and reached into his inner pocket. There was the letter from cousin Rose, but there was also a letter for him. A thrill moved through his chest as he studied the careful, looping script on the front that was swiftly becoming familiar.

Dear Wade,

All that you described in your last letter sounds so fascinating! Perhaps it's because I've been confined to the city for the majority of my life, but I'd very much like to know more about it.

He'd questioned himself when he'd put the advertisement in *The Matrimonial Times* a couple of months ago. It seemed strange to have to send off for a potential bride. Wade knew, however, that his only other choice was to marry the woman his mother had already picked for him. She had good intentions, but he wanted to be more in control of his life than that. The only way to stop Rita's badgering was to get married. If he was going to do that, he'd prefer that he at least have some say as to who the bride was.

The tack room was full of saddles and bridles, brushes and ointments. It was also the perfect place to tuck away a pen and ink along with a sheaf of papers, since his mother almost never came out here. He had a nice desk in the house, one that would be far more comfortable for writing letters than hunching on a stool and scrawling on an old board by lantern light, but then anything he did there was guaranteed to be discovered by his meddling mother.

Dearest Ella,

I'd be happy to explain more about my life as a rancher. At this point, however, I find it preferable to explain it all in person. Since I've enjoyed our correspondence so much, I'm officially extending my invitation for you to come to New Mexico before the holidays. I do find myself in need of a wife, and I believe the two of us make a fine match.

His mother wouldn't be pleased when she found out, but he'd deal with that when it came. This was his life, and he'd have to make her understand that. He'd bring a mail-order bride to the ranch, and Rita would have no choice but to leave him alone.

Chapter 3

Ella clasped the latest letter to her chest, pleasantly shocked by what it contained. A marriage proposal! She'd looked forward to each one of his letters, enjoying them as he described everything in such detail to her. It wasn't love, which was what she'd have preferred over everything. It couldn't be, since she'd never even met the man. But for once, it was her choice. This wasn't a dress that her mother had chosen for her or a school that her father had insisted she go to. It certainly wasn't a marriage to a dull, boorish man who would undoubtedly make her miserable. No, this was entirely her choice, and she knew she was going to make it.

Excitement rippled over her skin as she folded the letter and headed downstairs. She'd have to tell them right away, before they carried out any further wedding plans. This charade with Sheldon Jones had gone on long enough, but Ella hadn't yet discovered a way to tell them it wasn't happening. With Wade's letter, she could explain everything. The door to the library was closed. Ella pulled in a deep breath and lifted her hand to knock.

"Leonard, we really must discuss the food for the reception." Her mother's voice was distant through the thick wood.

Her father's sigh wasn't quite muffled enough for her to miss it. "Really, Rachel, isn't this the sort of thing you should be discussing with Ella?"

"I've tried, but we don't get anything done. Every time I bring up the wedding, she freezes up entirely and hardly says a word. Or if she does, she goes into such details about minor trivialities that we still have no decision by the end," Mrs. Price complained.

"Ha! She's still so dumbfounded by the excellent match I've made that she hardly knows how to talk about it!" The thwack that sounded through the door suggested that Mr. Price had slapped his knee.

"You never could understand women, Leonard. The girl doesn't want to marry Sheldon."

Ella's shoulders relaxed. Her mother knew! She could get out of this marriage without any excuses! She lifted her hand once more.

"But she'll come around in time," her mother continued, and Ella dropped her hand once again. "She's young and full of great notions, but once she's a little older she'll understand that this is a good match that will make her comfortable for the foreseeable future. Besides, it isn't as though she can back out."

Ella's stomach sank down to her slippers as she took a step away from the door. A lump formed in her throat. They weren't going to support her idea of moving to New Mexico, especially not to marry a stranger who was nothing more than a mere cattle rancher. They were going to stick by their decision and force her to marry Sheldon.

She hurried back up to her room and shut the door quietly behind her. She had to go before this got any further, and she had to go now. In a rush, she packed up a few precious items. Would they notice if she went out the side door? Would anyone see her and run to tell her parents that she was heading to the station? She hoped not.

Just before she left her bedroom for the very last time, Ella opened her desk drawer. She took out all the letters she'd received from Wade and stuffed them in her bag, and then she sat down to write. A quick missive to Wade would let him know she was on her way and might perhaps reach him before she did. For her parents, she left a much longer note.

The train ride was a long one, long enough that it had her questioning the distance she was creating between herself and the life she'd always known. The landscape changed regularly, with the trees thinning and the grass becoming more brown than green. The mountains were breathtaking, a sight she'd never have seen if she'd stayed home and married Sheldon Jones.

But as the train chugged into the southwest, she began to realize that this distance was precisely what would give her the independence she craved. Her father wouldn't be behind closed doors, directing her future as though she were nothing more than an investment. Her mother couldn't pretend that Ella was her little doll to dress up as she wished. This was *her* life now. She had the possibility for love and marriage, a greater chance for a happier future.

When the train made its final stop, Ella slowly stood. The platform was small, but it was bustling with people. She couldn't differentiate one from the other, and so she clutched her valise and waited while the train car emptied. This was it. This was the beginning of the rest of her life. She didn't know exactly what it would hold, and she had no experience living in a rough place such as this, but she had to go find out.

"Here you are, miss." The conductor kindly took her elbow. "Watch that last step. There you are."

"Thank you." The words barely came out, strangled by her nerves. She glanced around the platform, wishing she'd had more time. She'd been able to check the train schedule and let Wade know when she'd be arriving, but how would they ever find each other? The lump in her throat grew bigger as she looked around helplessly.

Suddenly, the crowd seemed to part. A tall man was striding toward her, his shoulders wide and a kindly smile on his face. He tipped his hat, revealing a mop of unruly blond hair over his stunning blue eyes. Ella had a sudden intake of breath as everyone around them dissolved, becoming little more than part of the background.

"Miss Price?"

Her ears were ringing. He was so handsome! Sheldon Jones was short and square, with a weak chin and a stray curl that could never quite be tamed with a comb. Wade Monroe was a stark contrast. He was tall and broad, with strong shoulders, and yet he moved with the grace of a gentleman. When he took her hand in introduction, she felt the callouses on his palm from his hard work. Though his pale hair was unruly under his hat and blew gently in the breeze, it suited the easy smile. "Yes," she finally managed. "And you must be Mr. Monroe."

He laughed lightly, a deep sound that pleased her. "I suppose we ought to call each other by our Christian names, since we already have in our letters."

That decision had felt like an intimate one at the time, one that her mother and her governess likely would've thought scandalous. Now, meeting him in person, it felt only right. In fact, everything suddenly felt right now that he was here. "I'd be happy to, Wade."

"Thank you, Ella."

Her name sounded beautiful from his lips, and Ella wondered if he could see the flush that had overtaken her cheeks.

"I'll get the rest of your luggage and load it in the wagon," Wade offered.

Reality dashed away the sense of romance and awe that she'd been feeling as Ella reached out a hand to stop him from moving toward the porters that were currently unloading the baggage car. "That won't be necessary. This is all I brought."

He lifted his brow, but he reached out to take it from her. "Then I suppose that saves me all the heavy lifting," he jested. "This way."

She took his offered elbow, finding that she could feel his strong muscles even through the material of his jacket. Ella bit her lip, wondering what he truly thought about her lack of luggage. She'd been honest in her explanation that her family had a decent income, and so it would only make sense that she'd have brought at least a trunk. In fact, Ella had told him quite a bit about her life. Sheldon Jones was the part she'd left out. She didn't want to go into a marriage with her new husband believing she'd only married him as a means of escape. The fact that it was true didn't deter her. It was important that they start with a clean slate, one in which they both had the best of intentions.

Wade put her valise in the back of his wagon and handed her up onto the seat. "Since I last wrote to you, I've been thinking.

We've only had a chance to get to know each other through a few letters. It's a very nice start, and one that I'm hopeful about. I thought, however, that we might both be happier if we were to have some time together before we said our vows."

She pursed her lips, worried about what this meant. "How would we do that?"

There was that lazy smile again. "It's very simple, really. My mother lives with me, and there's a spare bedroom. You could stay at the ranch with my mother as chaperone until we're married. What do you think?"

Ella felt that lump rising in her throat all over again. There was nothing wrong with the idea, really. It would give them each a chance to make sure they were suitable for each other, and it was just the sort of thing she would've wanted to do with any other man that she might marry. She'd had a whole lifetime to get to know Sheldon, and that had told her everything she needed to know. Truly, this was ideal.

And yet, it wasn't what she'd envisioned. Perhaps it wasn't realistic to think she might run out West, meet the man of her dreams, and race to the chapel. Still, she'd come with the idea of being married right away. What would her parents think of such an arrangement?

Just as that thought occurred to her, Ella reminded herself that she no longer cared what her parents thought. If she did, then she certainly wouldn't have taken a train to New Mexico. Her nerves were getting the better of her. She could turn around, get back on the train, and head straight back to Boston where she'd have to grovel for Sheldon to take her back. Or she could stay her with Wade and give this new relationship a try. She sent a silent prayer up that this would work out, that there was a reason she was here. "Yes, that sounds very nice."

Chapter 4

"My land starts right here, at this corner." Wade pointed to the split railing he'd put in himself around the front pasture. "This fence was one of the first things I put in when I claimed my land."

"Not before a home, surely," Ella protested.

Wade grinned. "Yes, actually. I just had a small, temporary shelter for a while. I needed a barn and a shed to work from before I could do anything else."

She blinked her big gray eyes, which had been eagerly drinking in the scenery during the wagon ride. "I can't even imagine."

"Well, don't worry," he said with a laugh. "Once I got through the first few months, I started work on a house. A real house, with floors and windows and everything. It's probably not as nice as where you lived back in Boston, but I find it comfortable enough."

"I'm sure it'll be just fine." She folded her hands in her lap and continued to look around, her dark hair shining in the sun. "I just can't get over how far I can see. I'm used to having buildings in every direction."

"You didn't get out of the city much?" The closest Wade had come to any kind of urban living was the small town where he'd grown up, but it had been little more than a gathering of a few buildings amongst the dust.

"Only when we went down to the waterfront to see the ships coming in or sailing out," she explained. "Looking out over the ocean like that isn't so different from here, really. Your eye just travels further and further into the distance.

"You'll get used to it," Wade assured her, and he truly hoped that she would. While his motivation for putting that advertisement in *The Matrimonial Times* hadn't been a completely honest one, he could see just how well it might work for him. He already knew from her letters that Ella Price was smart and interesting, but now he knew that she was quite beautiful, too. As soon as old Ida Ingram got word of this, both she and Rita would be in fits.

"Here we are." He turned up the driveway and parked the wagon in front of the barn. "I'll take you inside to get settled and to meet my mother, and then I'll give you a tour of the place."

"That sounds very nice, but I don't think it'll be necessary."

Wade whipped around, concerned. Had she come all the way out here and then decided she didn't want to stay, after all? He knew the ranch wasn't the most luxurious place in the country, but could she balk so quickly without seeing the inside of the house?

Ella was pointing her finger toward the house. Wade turned and saw his mother walking briskly up the path. She had a smile on her face, but he could tell it was pasted on.

He'd hoped to get Ella into the house first, but it was just as well that they got this conversation over with.

"Hello, Mother." He handed Ella down from the seat, and she landed lightly on the packed earth. "I was just coming up to see you."

Rita was still smiling. "I was in the kitchen, and I happened to look out the window when you drove up. I didn't know you were bringing company. Hello. My name is Rita Monroe. And you are?"

Ella blinked, and Wade's stomach clenched. He hadn't intended for Ella to have to tackle Rita Monroe on her own, but his mother had found a way to make sure she was in charge of the situation. He immediately regretted not filling Ella in on at least some of the situation, and he hadn't prepared his mother at all.

"Ella Price of Boston," his fiancée returned politely, taking hold of her skirt and dipping a perfect curtsy. "It's very nice to meet you."

"And it's nice to meet you as well, although it certainly would've been nice to have some warning so that I might have time to put together a nice dinner for all of us. As a matter of fact, I see that it's already getting rather late in the day, and we're quite far from town. Where will you be staying, Miss Price?"

"With us," Wade asserted, not wanting to leave poor Ella to handle his mother's sharp tongue on her own any longer. "Ella is my bride-to-be."

Rita's face froze, her smile smaller than it originally had been but still there. Only her eyes moved as they raked up and down Ella's body, taking in her stature, her dress, her looks, and probably other qualities that Wade hadn't thought to assess. "I see. And from Boston."

"Since we have the space, she'll be staying in the back bedroom. You can act as our chaperone while we spend some time together, until the wedding."

"The wedding." Rita's icy countenance was beginning to melt, but only to accommodate the fiery blaze of her eyes as she turned to her son. "Wade, do you have some time? I need to talk to you about a few things."

"Not at the moment, Mother. Ella has had a very long trip, and I'd like to get her settled into the house so that she has a chance to wash up and rest. If you'll excuse us." With Ella's valise in one hand, Wade offered his betrothed his elbow and brought her toward the house. Rita lagged a ways behind them.

Ella cleared her throat. "Wade, your mother seems rather surprised by my arrival. Did she not know that you intended to get married?"

"Oh, she knew," he assured her. Perhaps it wasn't to Ella, but still. "It's going to be a bit of an adjustment for her, that's all. Don't worry about it."

She pressed her lips together as her eyes fell toward the path under their feet. "I suppose it'll be an adjustment for all of us, won't it?"

"Yes, precisely," he eagerly agreed, happy that Ella had found a perspective that didn't make him look like a fool. It will all settle down in time."

Wade brought her into the house and showed her to her room. He left her to have some time alone and planned to slip back out to the barn. His mother, however, was waiting for him.

"Just what do you think you're doing?" she hissed, her fists on her hips and her brows angled down. "Who is this woman, and what are you playing at?"

He'd had enough of her intruding and her schemes, and it pleased him to know that he'd completely thrown her off with this unexpected visitor. "I'm not playing at anything. As I've explained to you, Ella and I are engaged."

Rita shook her head as her lips grew as tight as her purse strings. "You can't be!"

"We can, and we are." Wade was determined to remain calm. An argument between the two of them, especially one that happened so quickly on the heels of Ella's arrival, would only give Ella more reason to think there might be some problem with having her here.

"But where did she come from?" Mrs. Monroe spluttered.

He'd always loved and respected his mother, and a small part of him felt guilty for all of this, but Wade knew she'd never stop until she had no other choice. "She told you. Boston."

Rita's eyes grew wide with rage. "You know that's not what I mean!"

"You want to know everything? That's fine. I put an advertisement in *The Matrimonial Times,* a newspaper for—"

"You what?" Rita exploded. She clutched at her hair, her finger raking into the carefully created coif. "How could you do this to me?"

"I didn't do anything to you. I did this *for me*," he corrected. "You were the one who suggested—and that's a rather polite term for it—that I get married. And so I went and found myself a wife with the help of a newspaper and a few letters. Ella is a lovely young woman, as you can see, and so the problem has been solved. You no longer have to worry about your son finding a bride."

She pulled her hands from her hair, sending wild strands out in all directions. Now her fingers were tangled in her apron as she wrung it tightly. "But what about Tess? She'll be heartbroken!"

Wade had prepared himself for that. In fact, he'd been preparing for it for months. He knew that he and Tess simply weren't right for each other, and yet he'd watched the young woman for any signs that she might be interested in him. He wouldn't marry her simply to make his mother happy, but neither did he want to upset the girl. "No, she won't.

She doesn't have any more interest in marrying me than I do her."

"That's not true," Rita insisted. "Ida was just telling me the other day—"

"I'm not talking about Ida," he interrupted. "I'm talking about Tess. She's a nice girl, but she doesn't want to marry me. She only goes along with what her mother says because she doesn't want to upset her. I've been doing the same thing and for far too long. I should think you'd be able to see, now that my fiancée is right here in our house, that I'm putting my foot down."

"That's certainly one way to do it," Rita bit back.

"I think it was the only way." She could be angry with him if she wanted to be.

Wade knew she'd get past it, and then perhaps they'd have a chance at a peaceful, happy life.

Later that evening, Wade sat at the dinner table with his mother and his future wife. Rita had gone to great lengths to cook a wonderful meal, one far more intricate than any of their typical fare unless the preacher was coming over for supper.

"Your food is positively wonderful," Ella gushed. "I'm very impressed."

"Thank you," came Rita's cold reply. It was meant to impress, but Wade had a feeling it was also meant to intimidate. "Tell me, do you have much experience in the kitchen?"

Rita was wasting no time in testing her. Wade watched carefully, ready to jump in and interfere if need be, but so far Ella seemed capable of holding her own.

"I can't say that I do," she admitted with a smile, as though this weren't anything to be ashamed of. "I do look forward to learning, though."

"Hm." That was the only reply from Mrs. Monroe, who forced her fork through her potatoes with a bit too much force.

Wade lifted his napkin to his mouth to hide his grin. Ella didn't even realize that she was giving Rita a run for her money. His guess was that she was so used to handling Boston society that even the snidest comments were easy for her to handle. Wade had achieved much more with that little advertisement than he'd realized.

Chapter 5

Ella swiped her dust rag across the surface of the china cabinet in the dining room, carefully getting every corner and poking her finger into the little crevices of trim around the doors. She'd seen the maid do just this sort of thing many times, as well as beating the rugs or cleaning the windows, and yet she'd never given it much thought. Now that she had to actually participate in running a home, she was shocked to find just how quickly a layer of dust built up on every surface.

And yet, she was pleased to find that she didn't mind the work. It kept her busy, out here where there was no heavy social schedule that required her to show up and say nice things and look pretty just so that her family could stay in good standing with others. This was much more satisfying. It gave her a sense of accomplishment, of knowing that she'd actually done something with her day. Though she hadn't been on the Monroe ranch long, it gave her a promising feeling for the future.

She turned to the table, determined to get it as clean as possible before their dinner that night. She wanted to make a good impression on Mrs. Monroe, even if Wade's mother didn't seem all that thrilled with her. Ella wasn't sure what she might've done wrong or how she'd offended her, but neither did Rita give her any indication that she wanted to discuss it. Meanwhile, Ella used her training to keep her words polite and even, determined to make this arrangement work. There were times that she doubted the whole plan, but thoughts of a life with Sheldon Jones always had her changing her mind again.

The front door opened, admitting a chilly breeze. "Ella? There's a letter for you."

She dropped her dusting rag and rushed forward to get it, hoping that it might be a reply from Boston. Ella had written to her parents once she'd gotten settled in, informing them that she was safe and happy as she learned to navigate this new world. The postmark was from Boston, but the letter was from Bertie. "Thank you."

He gave her a polite nod before he moved off to the kitchen to speak with Rita.

Meanwhile, Ella hurried to her room and ripped open the seal.

I am so very excited about your new adventure! Though I miss you terribly, and I do wish that I still had you to cling to at the society events, I'm delighted to know that you'll have a happy future. I should also apologize, because I feel that I gave you some incorrect advice. We do need husbands to take care of us, but we shouldn't have to settle for ones that don't make us happy. Tell me, when are your nuptials set for? Though I'll be all the way back here in Boston, please know that I'll be thinking of you no matter the date!

Ella sat on her bed and tapped the corner of the letter on her chin. She'd been caught up in understanding how to live her new life here in New Mexico, and though she had certainly been thinking of her future married life to Wade, she hadn't given any specific thoughts to a wedding date. It had been a wonderful surprise when Wade had suggested they have a chance to get to know each other, one that she'd been happy to take advantage of, but just how long should they wait? Her reputation was in no danger as long as Rita was around, but it only made sense that they at least discuss the matter. Any marriage ceremony here would be far simpler than what she would've had in Boston, so there was no need to plan for months on end as Bertie was having to do, but Ella still wanted to know.

She tucked the letter away for the moment, wanting to have a little more information before she replied to Bertie. Ella stepped into the common space of the house, peering around to see where Wade had gone. She expected him to be at his desk, looking through the mail or checking his balance books. He'd dropped the rest of the mail he'd brought in on the surface of his desk, but he wasn't in the chair. Remembering that he'd headed toward the kitchen, she went there.

Rita glanced up sharply as she arrived. "What's the matter?"

"Nothing, really. I was just wondering if you knew where Wade had gone. I wanted to ask him a question." Ella stepped into the kitchen, lingering by the door. Rita was just one woman, and yet she seemed to be running the entire room with a remarkable efficiency. The pots simmering on the stove were regularly stirred. The bread in the oven came out perfectly golden, and the bird roasting over the fire was guaranteed to be crispy on the outside and juicy on the inside.

Rita shook her head while she scooped flour into a bowl. "I think he went back out to the barn."

"Oh. Perhaps I should go speak with him out there." Ella had been in the barn once or twice, since Wade had wanted to make sure she was familiar and comfortable with her surroundings, but the cooler winter weather and her household chores had mostly kept her indoors.

"I wouldn't," Rita grumbled. "He's busy."

"All right." Ella twisted her hands in front of her and frowned. Though Wade had been very kind and welcoming, the two of them had hardly spent any time together past those first few days. It was understandable that they would both be busy as they did the hard work of keeping the ranch running, but spending time apart meant they weren't getting to know each other like they were supposed to.

That was disappointing, but Ella wanted to make the best of everything she had here. "Is there anything I can do to help?"

"I'm getting things ready for Christmas. We're going to be donating some goodies for the children to have after their pageant at the town hall. You can help me with that."

"All right." Ella took her apron down from a hook on the wall and tied it around her waist. "What do I need to do?"

Rita paused, one hand leaning on the table. "You've never made cookies?"

Ella's eyes widened. She'd enjoyed them many times, but she didn't have a clue as to what actually went into making them. Ella had only spent as much time in the kitchen as her mother would allow, and that was very little. "I'm afraid not."

A few wrinkles of irritation passed over Rita's face, but she handed Ella a bowl. "Crack four eggs into this."

Ella swallowed nervously. It was only the first step, and already it was something that she'd never done at all. She picked an egg from the basket on the table and tried to remember what she'd seen their cook do back at home. One quick bang on the side of the bowl sent the shell into splinters and the goo inside running down the outside of the bowl.

Rita sighed. "You don't even know how to crack an egg?"

"I'll just try again." She knew she could do this. She *had* to be able to do this. Rita wouldn't always be around to cook and clean, and Ella needed to learn as much as she could. Using a little less forced this time, she cracked the egg again and made a nice crevice in the shell. Her thumbs jammed straight into it when she tried to open the shell the rest of the way, but at least everything went where it was supposed to.

The rest of the batch of cookies went much the same, with Ella feeling completely lost in every step and Rita irritated that she knew so little. What pleased Ella the most, however, was knowing that these cookies would be going to a wonderful cause. It made her think about all the wonderful Christmases she'd had back home. It had always been a joy to buy gifts for friends, to attend parties, and to give to charities. It wouldn't be the same out here, but the spirit was still there.

That spirit continued when Wade finally returned just before dinner, dragging a spruce tree behind him. "I've got the tree!" he announced.

"Put it up in the corner," Rita directed.

"How lovely!" Ella stood back and watched, thrilled that they would have such a wonderful sign of the holidays right there in the living room. The scent was already filling the air. "What do we have to decorate it with?"

"Anything you'd like," Wade replied. "I was always a big fan of popcorn garland as a child."

"That's only because you ate all the popcorn off of it," his mother reminded him. "I've got a few baubles. I'll go get them."

The three of them passed the evening swiftly as they prepared for the holiday. Wade put the popcorn over the fire. Ella threaded a needle and began creating the garland, though she noticed Rita's watchful eye as she did so. They decorated the tree with bits of ribbon, candles, pinecones, nuts, and berries until it looked like a cornucopia of all their blessings.

"Wade, can you put this up at the top?" Ella asked, finding that she couldn't quite reach the upper branches.

"Of course." He took the little bow she'd made out of a scrap of ribbon, his finger brushing hers, and reached above her head to perch it right near the top of the tree. He stood back to study his work and then smiled at her. "How's that?"

"Perfect." Her heart fluttered every time he smiled at her like that, as if she was the only other person in the room. It made her feel special, and it helped erase any regrets about leaving Boston. She could never love Sheldon Jones, but there was a chance she could love Wade. She hadn't forgotten that she wanted to talk to him about their wedding, but Rita was buzzing around them like a bee. It would have to wait for another day, and right now she would simply enjoy the moment.

Chapter 6

Wade turned up his collar against the chilly wind. While the area was hot and dry much of the year, the winters were chilly and somber. He looked up from the fence line he'd been checking to take in the scope of his land. He was proud of all that he'd accomplished here, starting from nothing and building it up into an actual homestead. He'd put every single fence post in by hand, and he'd scraped out the foundation for the barn. Some local boys had helped him to erect it, and in exchange he'd helped them with buildings on their own properties, as well. He'd built a working ranch as well as a sense of community, and Wade knew none of them could get through it all without each other.

He'd lived rough until it was time to build the house, the final structure that would ensure his permanent deed on the land. He'd wanted to wait until he had the time and the resources to do it well, and he could look down the hill at it now and be proud of it. A curl of smoke rose from the chimney, and he knew he'd have a hot meal and a comfortable bed waiting for him when he returned from his work.

Apparently, he also had company. A wagon was parked in the barnyard, and it wasn't his. Wade nudged his heels against his horse and hurried down the hill to see what was happening.

Wade entered the house cautiously and was greeted by the sounds of clinking pots and pans and feminine laughter. He was relieved for a moment, knowing there had been no danger to his mother and fiancée while he'd been gone, but then he recognized the voice that floated to him out of the kitchen.

"Rita, dear, it was so *kind* of you to invite us to dinner. Ever since George died, the holidays simply haven't been the same, and it feels so good to have friends around."

"Now, Ida, there's no need for you girls to stay at home and feel sorry for yourselves at such a joyous time of year. We're not just friends. Wade and I consider you to be like family!"

That relief quickly dissolved. Ida was here, and no doubt Tess was as well. His mother hadn't said a word to him about any such arrangement, though any other time she'd invited them over she'd gone on and on about it for days in advance. Wade knew precisely what this meant, and he stepped into the kitchen.

The scene before him looked perfectly innocent. The two older women were standing at the stove, laughing and chatting. Ella and Tess were seated at the kitchen table with mugs of tea in their hands, smiling politely. Did Ella have any clue what was happening here? Did she understand that Tess had been pushed in front of Wade's face at every opportunity until now? She smiled sweetly at him, and he decided that she didn't know or at least had decided that she didn't want to.

"Wade! You're back early!" his mother exclaimed. "How nice! It'll be just a little bit until supper is ready."

He nodded politely at their visitors before his eyes landed on his mother again. "That's fine. Could I speak to you for a moment?"

"I'm rather busy with the meal," Rita reminded him.

"You go on." Ida brushed a hand at Rita. "I'll mind the roast. It isn't as though I haven't made plenty of them over the years!"

"Wade, you can help me set the table." Rita gave him a hard look as she passed by him and went out the kitchen door.

He could hardly wait until they reached the dining room. "Just what do you think you're doing?" he demanded.

"Setting the table," Rita replied innocently.

"Mother, I know what your intentions have always been when you've invited the Ingrams over before. I can't believe you would do this while Ella is here!" He'd thought for sure she'd stop with her meddling as soon as his new bride arrived, but he'd clearly been wrong. Rita would go as far as she wanted to in order to get her way.

"Who says I'm doing anything?" She set a stack of plates on the table. "Ida is an old friend of mine. Are you going to stand there and say that I can't invite her and her daughter over for a nice meal around the holidays? As a matter of fact, it seems that Tess and Ella are getting along nicely."

"Only because both of them are too polite to do anything else." He couldn't even imagine what Ida and Tess must've thought when his mother introduced Ella as his fiancée. There was a good chance Ida had been in on the whole thing, however.

"We're all here to have a nice meal, Wade. There's no need for you to make a fuss." She pulled out the good silverware.

He stiffened his shoulders, ready to continue arguing, but he realized it wouldn't do any good. She would dig in her heels until she got what she wanted, and she didn't care who she hurt along the way. That was fine. He could fight just as hard. "Very well." He left to wash up.

Wade was prepared by the time his mother called him in for dinner. He was the first to the dining room, where he held out a chair politely as he smiled at his fiancée. "Ella, I'd be honored if you'd sit here across from me."

"Why, thank you," she said breathlessly, taking her seat.

He noticed that she smelled of cinnamon, and as he sat down he noticed she was looking quite nice tonight. Wade doubted she'd had any extra time to get ready, because part of Rita's scheme would be to spring the Ingrams on Ella just as much as she had on Wade, but the ringlets of dark hair that framed her face fell delicately against her cheek. "This looks like a wonderful dinner."

"It's sure to be," Rita agreed, "especially because of these wonderful rolls that Tess made. They're so light and fluffy, and that's not a task that's easily done. It requires lots of patience and talent. You should try one, Wade."

He had no choice, considering they were all watching him. Wade set it on his plate but didn't touch it. "What about you, Ella? Did you have time to contribute? I know you've been putting a lot of work into making the house look so nice for the holidays."

She flushed and batted her lashes. "I have done quite a bit of dusting, but I did roast the vegetables. It's still something I'm learning, but I think they came out all right."

Wade immediately scooped a spoonful onto his plate. Truthfully, he expected them to be terrible. It was obvious from the moment Ella had arrived that she'd never done any of the sort of work their lifestyle required, and she'd been honest with him about growing up as a socialite. He found, however, that the vegetables only lacked a bit of salt. "They're very good."

"Thank you." She looked down at her lap shyly.

"Tess, you should tell Wade about all the work you've been doing with the children to prepare them for their Christmas play." Rita turned to Wade. "Did you have any idea that she volunteers with the church regularly? And in quite a few of their programs, too."

"It's nothing, really," Tess replied.

"Certainly, it is!" Rita countered. "Why, those little ones wouldn't have a Christmas play without you. It means so much to them, as it does to their families who get to come and see it. They all have a wonderful time, and your service is a true boon to the community."

Wade allowed himself a moment to chew his roast. He ignored his mother's overture while he thought. He'd tried telling her that he didn't want to marry Tess. He'd even brought home another woman to prove his point, and yet Rita still seemed set on singing Tess's praises all evening. Was there anything he could say that would make her understand his intentions?

He set his fork down slowly and took a drink of the wine his mother had poured for this special occasion. As he looked into the dark liquid, he knew precisely what he needed to do.

Wade rose from his chair and lifted his glass. It took only a moment for everyone to look in his direction, and he smiled politely. "I propose a toast to this cozy holiday season, as well as having family and friends together. In fact, since you're all here, I have an announcement to make. Ella and I will be married by Christmas."

Ella leaned back in surprise, her fingers fluttering near the neckline of her deep green gown, but she gave him a sweet smile.

Ida blinked as she looked back and forth at the other dinner guests. "Well, now! I had no idea!"

Rita merely gasped and crumpled her napkin in her fist.

Tess straightened in her chair, her eyes alight. She grabbed her glass and lifted it. "To the happy couple! Congratulations!" She clinked her glass with Wade's.

As he slid back down into his seat, Wade knew he had won.

Later that evening, however, he wasn't so sure. Their guests had gone and the house was silent. He'd worked all day, and there was more work waiting for him in the morning. After the rather eventful dinner, he ought to be exhausted, and yet he tossed and turned under the quilt. Finally, unable to watch the moon trace a slow path through the sky any longer, he rose.

Wade slipped through the front door and out onto the front porch. He stepped up to the railing, ignoring the chill through his shirt sleeves as he looked up at the moon. The soft glow highlighted all that he'd built here on his ranch, all that he'd worked so hard for. It lighted the roofline of the barn and the top rails of the fences, while deep shadows lingered around the back side of the tool shed and under the trees. It was a scene that was incredibly familiar to him, one he could see even with his eyes closed, and yet it looked completely different now that he was about to marry Ella.

"It's beautiful, isn't it?"

Startled, Wade turned. Ella was just at the other end of the porch, though he hadn't turned to look when he'd walked out. Even now, she was almost invisible in the dark shadows under the porch roof. "Come here."

She rose and came to him on silent feet. Her dressing gown was pulled tightly around her, and when he took her hands, he could tell that she'd been out here for quite some time. Wade looked into her eyes, which picked up the silvery light as though they themselves were made of the same stuff as the moon. He saw so many questions in those eyes, ones that she didn't dare speak aloud. Had he meant all that he'd said tonight? Why had he so suddenly become interested in marrying her, and why so quickly? What had *really* happened at that dinner table that she didn't understand?

Wade found there were plenty of questions bubbling up inside of him as well.

Had he treated Ella poorly by suddenly giving her such fawning affection? And why had he been distancing himself from her so much until tonight? He knew those answers, and he wouldn't speak them aloud, either.

He also knew that this was the woman who was about to be his wife. Overwhelmed by conflicting emotions, he went with the one that felt the strongest. Wade pulled her close and pressed a kiss to her lips. She tensed with surprise before she melted into his embrace, soft and comfortable in his arms. He held her there, with only the moon to see.

Chapter 7

"We don't have any gifts for Christmas. What are we going to do?" Seven-year-old Charlotte Brown waved her hands in the air in mock despair while several of the adults in the audience suppressed their laughs.

Wade managed a glance to his right at his fiancée. Was it just a figment of his imagination, or had the two of them grown closer since that shared, secret kiss? Every time he looked at her, even when it was just through the corner of his eye, he could see just how beautiful she was. It baffled him that she didn't have every man in Boston asking for her hand, and he was fortunate that she'd made the decision to come to New Mexico. She laughed at a joke from the stage, though

Wade had missed it because he'd been too busy studying the way her smile made her glow.

He turned his eyes back toward the front of the room. Tess stood just to the side of the stage, waiting in the wings to give the children their cues if they missed them. She was happy and pleasant in her own element here, focused on the children. She encouraged them and praised them. Tess was an honorable woman, and one that plenty of men would be happy to make their wife. He could understand why his mother thought she was such an eligible bride, but he simply didn't feel that same swelling of excitement in his chest when he looked at her.

Twisting slightly to his left, Wade cast a look at his mother on the other side. She sat with her back ramrod straight and her hands folded in her lap. A deep frown etched lines that stretched from the side of her nose down to her jaw. That was the same look she'd had on her face ever since his announcement at dinner a few nights ago. Wade had expected her to pull him aside and give him an earful, and he'd been ready to respond, and yet Rita hadn't done anything of the sort. She'd distanced herself from him, going about her work without hardly a word. Wade knew this was a punishment from her. Did he deserve it? He'd wanted her to stop but hadn't wanted anyone to get hurt.

"Merry Christmas!" the children announced from the stage, bowing and causing a huge round of applause from the audience. Wade was startled back into the present moment.

With the play finished, the chairs were pushed back along the edges of the room. The town hall was bustling with activity as the children played games. It was just as much of a show for the adults as the play had been, as they always had such a fantastic time. Rita headed off to help set out the food.

Ella watched her go, biting her lip slightly. "I think I'll see if Tess needs any help."

Wade turned to look at her, surprised that she would so willingly assist Tess. Then again, Tess had been the first one to raise her glass at dinner. Tess wasn't the problem. If Ella understood there was a problem at all, then she also understood that it wasn't Tess's fault. "That's nice of you."

"I hear that lovely young lady is about to be your bride," Jacob Green said as he came up alongside Wade. He was one of the men who'd helped Wade with the heavier duties of building his ranch, and the two of them had often assisted each other. "She must be quite the woman, indeed, if your mother has approved of this."

Wade frowned.

"Oh. I see," Jacob responded, understanding even without a word. "Although I can't see why. Unless perhaps your bride has some terrible temper that she doesn't put on display when she comes to church or goes into town, then I don't see any reason why Rita would be upset."

"She'll be upset with anyone who isn't Tess Ingram," Wade replied, knowing his conversation was safe with Jacob. "She's set her cap on me marrying her best friend's daughter; even though I've told her many times that I'm not interested. Tess is a nice girl, but she's not for me."

"I've an inkling she feels the same way," Jacob noted.

Wade turned to face him fully. "What do you mean?"

His friend pointed at the back corner of the room. "You've got all the evidence you need right there."

Wade looked. Tess was standing next to William Adams, who smiled warmly at her as he spoke. Wade couldn't hear what was said, but it was obvious by the look on Tess's face that she was enjoying the conversation.

Her hands were clasped behind her back, and she slightly swung her shoulder back and forth as she listened attentively. She looked like a schoolgirl, enchanted by a handsome older boy. She'd never looked at Wade like that, and he knew that Jacob was right. "I'm glad to see it. I would never want to hurt Tess, and I even think she and Ella could become friends if my mother didn't have anything to say about it."

"Where did you find Miss Price, anyway? I don't remember seeing her around."

"She's here all the way from Boston." Wade explained just how the two of them had met.

Meanwhile, one of the children had found a book of poetry and was waving it in the air at Ella. "Read to us!"

"Me?" Flattered, Ella pressed a hand to her chest. "Certainly. Let's find a comfortable place to sit." She pulled up a chair while all the children gathered around her. Opening the book and flipping through a few pages, she smiled when she found the one she wanted. Ella read aloud in a beautiful voice, eloquent and sure. In that moment, if he just squinted a little, Wade could imagine that she was in a ballroom in the city instead of a simple town hall in the middle of nowhere.

"Yes, that's quite a lady," Jacob said when she was done. He clapped Wade on the shoulder. "I'll see you at the grange hall."

Left alone, Wade watched as the children asked Ella for another poem. They watched her eagerly as she read, captivated by her performance. She really was quite a lady, and it was evident to him now that she didn't belong in a little town in New Mexico. Her delicate hands weren't used to the hard work required of a rancher's wife. In fact, she deserved a much finer living than Wade could ever give her. She certainly deserved to be treated with respect and dignity. Wade knew he could do better by her, but would his mother ever come to think of her as a daughter?

The announcement he'd made about their wedding had been a spontaneous one, though it hadn't been ingenuine. Only a handful of people had witnessed it, and yet Wade had every intention of standing by his promise. He couldn't help but wonder, though, if perhaps Ella deserved a much better husband than him.

Chapter 8

"Get that bacon out of the pan before you burn it."

Ella peered at the crackling strips of meat in the cast iron skillet. "I didn't think they looked quite done."

"They still cook a bit after you take them out because of the hot grease. Wade doesn't like his bacon too crispy," Rita replied bitterly.

"All right." Ella did as she was told, carefully removing the bacon and trying not to burn herself on the sizzling grease. The longer she spent here and the more time she spent in the kitchen, she realized just how much she'd taken advantage of all the wonderful meals she'd eaten at home. She'd never truly taken the time to consider how much time and effort had gone into each one, even when it was a simple plate of eggs and bacon.

She'd finished just as Wade came into the kitchen, and she turned to him with a smile. "Good morning. Breakfast is ready."

They usually had their morning meals in the kitchen to keep things simpler, but Wade didn't pull out a chair. "Thank you, but I'm not hungry this morning."

Ella glanced down at the bacon. "Is it too crispy?"

Some emotion moved over his face that she couldn't quite identify. Sadness? Hurt? "No. Nothing like that. I'll eat later. I'm going into town today, and I'm in a hurry." Taking only a mug of coffee, he left to finish getting ready for the day.

She worried for him when he'd left. He hadn't eaten breakfast, nor had he taken any food for the drive to town and back. He was a grown man and would surely stop at the inn when he felt the need to eat, but it still bothered her. Ella was starting to think it just might have something to do with her, and a sense of worry was beginning to build in the pit of her stomach.

In the afternoon, when Rita insisted there was nothing to do in the kitchen and the rest of the housework was caught up, Ella sat by the fire in the living room. She slowly wove her needle in and out of the bit of fabric caught in a hoop, practicing a few stitches.

Ella had always been more interested in reading and painting than she had in needlework. As her mother saw these as perfectly acceptable hobbies, she was encouraged to pursue them. She could see, however, that they were not very useful in a place like this.

The door opened, and the wind slammed it back against the wall with a bang. Ella jumped, stabbing the needle through her finger. She yanked it back, leaving a small red dot to stain her hard work. "Hello, Wade. Did you have a nice visit to town?"

"It was fine." He reached into his jacket pocket and withdrew an envelope. "The postmaster had decided that you're very popular. He said nobody else gets quite as many letters as you do."

"Thank you." It was still warm from his body, where he'd kept it protected on the long drive home. Her fingers clenched slightly as she recognized the handwriting.

Wade had started to turn away, but he paused. "Is everything all right?"

Ella knew there was so much she should discuss with him. She should ask him exactly what had happened the night Ida and Tess had come over and why the older women had behaved so oddly. She should talk to him about his own behavior, as well. He'd waffled back and forth between being warm and friendly to completely standoffish. Ella didn't know if it was something she'd done or if this was simply how he was, and she ought to find out before she officially became Mrs. Monroe. It all boiled up inside of her, desperate to come out, and yet she couldn't get any of it past her teeth. She was too scared of what the truth might be, that coming to New Mexico might all have been a grand mistake.

"Yes," she finally managed. "Everything is fine. I just pricked myself with a needle, that's all."

Wade went about his business, and Ella returned to her seat by the fire. She'd been anticipating a letter from her parents, and it had finally arrived. As nervous as she was about her future with Wade, she also dreaded what this letter might contain. She knew she'd disappointed them with her actions, and there was no doubt that abandoning her engagement to Sheldon had caused some gossip amongst their peers. The Prices were

undoubtedly ashamed. What would she do if
Wade chose not to marry her? She couldn't
possibly go back, not after the way she'd left.

She broke the seal and unfolded the
pages within. Remarkably, the letter smelled
faintly of her mother's perfume. Ella took a
deep breath and began to read.

Dearest Ella,

*We're in receipt of your letter, and
we're glad to know that you've arrived at
your destination safely. We've worried about
you greatly ever since your departure. I had
to ask your father to show me the New Mexico
Territory on a map, and it's shockingly far
from our dear old Boston.*

*I must tell you that we were shocked
and angered by your disappearance. Though*

I suspected that you weren't delighted with the arrangement, I never thought it would make you so unhappy that you'd leave. Please know that your father and I only wanted what we thought was best for you.

It turns out—and I'm ashamed to admit it—that we were completely wrong. Sheldon Jones has been implicated in a rather scandalous affair regarding a maid in the Ellis household. I can assure you that the busybodies instantly stopped talking about your actions once they heard of his. I'm terrified to think of what might have happened if you had stayed and if we might not have discovered Sheldon's true colors until after you had wed.

With all of that said, please know that we still want only what is best for you. We

*love you, regardless of any and all
circumstances. You're always welcome to
come home, and indeed we hope that you and
your new husband might find time to visit us
at some point in the future. I look forward to
hearing from you again, and it's my most
sincere hope that we can continue to at least
reach out to each other through letters even if
we are apart. Your father sends his love.*

A teardrop fell on the edge of the letter,
and Ella quickly blotted it away before it
smudged the ink. Perhaps she hadn't been so
wrong to get out of her betrothal to Sheldon,
but at what cost? She was all the way on the
other side of the country now. The man she'd
intended to marry would hardly look her in
the eye or speak to her. His mother treated
her as though she was a pest in the house, a
mouse she had to tolerate because she was

unable to catch it and throw it outside. What kind of a life was that? Was that what her parents wanted for her? More to the point, was that what she wanted for herself?

Ella looked up at the Christmas tree. It had delighted her so much when Wade had first brought it in, and she'd been so excited to spend the holidays here. Now, she could only think of all the celebrations and toasts that she was missing back home. The mantel was undoubtedly laden with a garland of evergreen, and another one would have been carefully wound around the banister. Everyone would put on their best coats and their warmest boots and get out in the cold only to warm up at the fire of a friend or family member. The neighbors would lift their hands and call out 'Merry Christmas' when they happened to see each other outside.

All the shops would be filled to the brim with various gifts. Ella and Bertie would have gone around to each one of them to decide what to buy.

Those memories made her current situation suddenly feel forlorn. Her engagement to Sheldon had been a problem. Instead of facing it, Ella had run away from it. She could justify it all now, knowing as she did that Sheldon was an even worse match than she'd realized, but she'd gone about it in the wrong way. Ella had wanted to feel independent, to know that she was making her own decisions for her own life, but she'd acted like a spoiled child.

Now what was she to do?

She glanced toward the door, wondering where Wade had gone. She remembered the man who'd greeted her when she'd first stepped off the train. He'd been everything she'd hoped for and more. She'd seen the excitement in his eyes, and she'd known that there was a true chance for them. Was that man still there inside him? Christmas was only a couple of days away, and yet Wade hadn't said another word about wedding plans. Perhaps he'd never truly meant it after all.

Chapter 9

The sun had started to climb in the New Mexico sky. The day was set to be a chilly one regardless, and Ella tugged her shawl a little tighter around her shoulders. The winter weather here simply wasn't the same as it was back home. She missed the snow, but she also knew that the lack of it made her life a bit easier. At least she wasn't mopping muddy puddles off the floor every morning.

She glanced toward the barn. It was early still, but she knew Wade was already gone. Ella knew little of exactly what he did while he was out on horseback all day, checking the fence and moving around the cattle. It wasn't work she was made for, and she knew that, and yet she longed to ask him to take her with him. She just wanted to see what he did, to be a part of his experience, to understand things from his perspective.

Was that foolish? She was beginning to think so. Ella sighed and leaned on the porch railing, just a few feet from where Wade had kissed her a few nights ago. That had been such an unexpected pleasure. It had made her heart jump and her skin warm. She'd felt a rush of excitement and love, but a great amount of confusion had followed it. Wade didn't seem able to make up his mind about her. Could she blame him, since her own conclusions wavered so much?

In general, she knew he was a good man. He worked hard. He went to church and cared about his community. Everyone who saw him lifted their hands to wave hello or stopped to chat. He was polite. Even Tess had told him what a wonderful match the two of them made and had offered her profuse congratulations, though Ella suspected something was happening there that she didn't understand. Was Tess merely covering up her true emotions because she'd hoped to marry Wade herself?

And if she did, would that be better for Wade?

The mere thought of him being with someone else made her heart ache, despite the fact that he'd already promised to marry her. Ella cared for him. She wanted to find a future with him, but she didn't know how.

The door opened and closed behind her. "There you are. You're supposed to be bringing in firewood."

Ella glanced down at the wood carrier that sat next to her feet. Yes, she'd had a reason for coming out here, a practical one, but her mind and heart had distracted her. "I'll get back to it in a moment."

Rita let out an impatient sigh, a noise that had become quite familiar to Ella at this point. The older woman didn't seem happy with anything she did, no matter how hard she tried. The door opened and closed again, but the sound of footsteps told Ella that she still wasn't alone.

"You're not meant for Wade."

Ella turned and looked straight into Rita's eyes. They were the same dark blue as Wade's, though there was a completely different light in them. His had a tendency to show compassion, warmth, or hurt. Rita's always looked stony and angry, as they did right now.

Her throat clenched around the impolite words that threatened to rise up. Ella had been raised to always be polite and generous, to give everyone the benefit of the doubt no matter how awful they were. It had gotten her through many a dinner party and ball, when those of Boston society decided they had something particularly judgmental to say. It could even be a little fun to smile at them and offer a reply that left them wondering if they'd been snubbed or agreed with. She'd done her best to ignore Rita's attitude so far, and she wouldn't be outright rude to her, but Ella knew she had to be more direct. "Why do you say that?"

Mrs. Monroe snorted and waved her hand around her as if the yard and the buildings around it held all the answers. "Isn't it obvious? Surely you've seen just how much hard labor goes into working this land. We rise early to get things started, and we work hard throughout the day. There are certain times of year—like calving season—when we're up all night. Even so, we have to push through when the sun rises again. This life will put callouses on your hands and feet, and scars everywhere else. Then, even when you know you've toiled away and put everything you possibly can into it, a disease can come through your herd and wipe away everything you've done."

"Then why would anybody do it?" Ella dared to ask.

"Why?" Rita repeated. "Why? How can you even ask yourself that? You said your father was in shipping. Why would he see the need to load a boat up with everything that America has to offer and send it off to Europe? Why would anybody come claim land on the frontier? Because it's hard work that's worth doing, that's going to change things for future generations. That doesn't mean that it's for everyone, though."

"Perhaps not, but I don't think anyone comes West without having to learn a thing or two. I've already leaned quite a bit in the short time that I've been here. I'll continue to learn, as well. I might be young, but that just means I have plenty of time to figure it out." It was the closest thing to an argument that she'd offered Rita since she arrived, and she waited for the older woman's retaliation.

Rita's eyes narrowed. "You actually believe that, don't you? It just goes to show how much of a fool you truly are. Ella, you come from a well-to-do family in the city. You haven't had to work a day in your life beyond picking out the color of your next gown or deciding whose tea party you'll be attending. You don't understand what true hardship is. There's a certain lifestyle that you're used to, and it isn't this one."

Though Rita was determined to drive her out, Ella was just as set on proving her wrong. "I can't help what life I was born into, but that doesn't mean I can't choose for myself for the future." In fact, that was precisely why she was here. She wanted a chance to make her own decisions. If she had to pay some consequences, then so be it. That was better than moving through her days as someone else's pawn.

"Then I suggest you learn to choose with a bit of wisdom. A few weeks out here is nothing compared to months and years. You're going to be miserable, and that means you're going to make Wade miserable. Wade needs a wife. Not just a pretty little thing on his elbow when he shows up at the church or the town hall, not a woman like you who just costs time and money. He needs someone who can roll up her sleeves and dig into this earth, who can give him robust children and keep going. You're only torturing him."

Ella gaped at her, shocked that she would blatantly say such hateful things. Even the worst of the gossips back in Boston wouldn't dare to be so bold. But then again, this was precisely what Rita had been trying to tell her ever since she'd arrived. With her looks, and her tone, and her cold shoulder, she'd been telling Ella all along that she didn't belong here and she wasn't wanted. Suddenly, all the fight drained out of her. "Perhaps you're right." With a swish of her skirt, she turned and went into the house.

She couldn't stop the tears that flowed down her cheeks and dripped off her chin, nor did she try. This whole charade had been ridiculous. She'd been mindless enough to believe that she and Wade might actually love each other, that they might make a good marriage and create a happy family. She'd thought she was running away from her problem in Boston, but the truth was that she'd only created another one. She'd saved herself from the dismal life she was bound to have with Sheldon, but in that process she'd only made things worse for Wade. The man needed a wife, as his mother had said. It just wouldn't be her.

She closed the door to her room, forcing herself not to slam it. Rita had already won, and there was no need to let her believe that Ella was completely out of control. She pulled the valise from under the bed and used the edge of her apron to wipe off the bit of dust that had accumulated on it since her arrival. She hadn't brought much, and she wouldn't be leaving with anything more. Ella was glad now that she hadn't brought a trunk full of her fine clothes, because now she didn't have to find a way to lug it out of here. It was a bright spot in her day, but it was still incredibly dim.

Taking a moment to clean her face, Ella knew there was nothing else she could do. She picked up her bag and lifted her chin, keeping her shoulders straight as she walked out the front door. She glanced toward the barn, but she already knew Wade wasn't there. Should she wait until she could explain? No. That would mean hours more in the same house with Rita, and Ella simply couldn't stand for that. His mother would explain everything. She would only speak the truth from her own perspective, but Ella had to leave her to that. Nothing she said would change their circumstances, regardless.

Ella turned to her right and began the long walk into town. She could feel the growing distance between herself and the place that she'd come to think of as home. Now it never would be. Ella would be forced to test the contents of her mother's letter. Would she truly be accepted when she came home? Or had Mrs. Price only said such nice things because she believed that Ella was wed and happy in New Mexico? If so, then Ella had no idea what she would do or where she would turn. She had to hope that she at least had a few friends left in the world.

The cold was beginning to bite through her cloak when she heard a wagon drawing up alongside her. A small bubble of hope rose in her as she thought it might be Wade, coming after her to bring her back home, but it was Jacob Green. He slowed the wagon to a halt and tipped his hat. "Good morning, Miss Price. It's rather a chilly day to be out for a walk. Can I take you back home?"

"Thank you, but I'm actually going into town."

He eyed her valise, and his brow wrinkled. "I'm actually headed into town myself. I'll save you a few steps." Jacob held out his wide hand.

Ella considered refusing, even though she knew Jacob to be a kind man and one of Wade's good friends. She'd met Mrs. Green at the Christmas play and had enjoyed her company, pleased to know there would be such good people around her as she started her wedded life. The only reason she wanted to turn him down was because she was feeling sorry for herself, however, and it wouldn't do her any good if she died from exposure before she ever even saw the church steeple over the horizon.

Jacob drove on for a while before he spoke again. "I won't pry into your business, Miss Price, but I will say I know that things can be difficult when it comes to working out a marriage. I think Mrs. Green would've been just as happy to kill me as to kiss me when we were first wed and she realized what an oaf I could be."

"That's hard to believe," Ella said, allowing herself a small smile. It was still cold here in the wagon, but at least they moved along much more swiftly.

"Oh, it's true," he assured her. "She swore my brain was made of rocks, but she managed to make me see the error of my ways. In fact, I think it's safe to say she's the one who made me into the man I am today.

All I'm trying to say is that it's not always easy, but sometimes it's still worth it."

"I appreciate that, Mr. Green, but I simply can't stay where I'm not wanted."

He leaned back in surprise. "Well. I guess we've both heard something that's hard to believe today."

"Thank you. I don't mean to get you involved in Wade's business, so please don't mind me." She looked away and clamped her teeth over her tongue, knowing Rita would have even more to say about her once she realized Ella had gone and told someone else her problems.

"Don't you worry. I won't say a thing if that's the way you want it." He pulled into town and slowed down. "I have to ask, though, are you sure I shouldn't go rustle up Wade and bring him to come and see you? There's a lot the two of you might be able to work out over a nice meal at the inn."

"Thank you, but no. Really, I think it's much better if nothing more is said." She stepped down from the wagon and looked up imploringly.

Jacob pressed his lips together and looked like he wanted to protest, but he shook his head. "I'll do as you ask, Miss Price. Do be careful."

"I will." She took her valise when he handed it down to her and headed into the station.

Chapter 10

Wade stepped out of the barn and headed toward the house. He jammed his hands into his pockets and gritted his teeth together as he glanced ahead, checking to see if Ella had finished her regular morning routine of bringing in the firewood. There was no sign of her, and he relaxed a little bit. Wade knew he shouldn't, but he'd fallen back into the habit of avoiding her as much as possible around the ranch. He'd taken note of her habits and her routine so that he could slip in and out of the house or barn without ever coming into view and hopefully without giving her any indication of just what he was doing. It meant that he didn't have to face the reality that he'd created for himself. He'd promised himself to this woman, and he wasn't a man who broke his promises. He knew, however, that he truly didn't deserve her. How could he stand in the sight of God and make a vow to a marriage that shouldn't be happening in the first place?

He normally would've made enough excuses to himself to stay out in the fields or at least the barn for several more hours, but the wind was picking up and there was truly no other work for him to do right now. The herd was so well taken care of that they probably wondered why he was still spending any time with them. Wade had finally reached a point where he could no longer hide. What would he do when he went inside and inevitably ran into his fiancée? Would he find the courage to speak to her?

But as he stepped up onto the porch, he noticed that the neat stack of firewood didn't look any smaller than it had when he'd left the house earlier that morning. Was Ella running behind? Inside, he checked the living room. There was no sign of her in the chair that she preferred close to the fire. The sewing basket—which Mrs. Green had put together for her—sat neatly closed next to it. Wade next moved to the dining room, wondering if perhaps his mother had once again set her to polishing the spoons that didn't need it or wiping invisible dust from the hutch. He'd been suspecting that Rita was finding things for Ella to do not because they needed to be done but so that she'd be out of the way. The dining room was empty.

His mother's angry voice wasn't coming through the kitchen door, ordering

Ella around, so he didn't think she was in there. Still, he decided to check. Rita sat alone at the kitchen table. The stove was cold, and there were no signs of any meal preparation around her. She clutched her hands together against her head as she looked down at the table, but she looked up with a start when he arrived. "Wade."

Something was definitely wrong. "Where is she?"

She swiped a hand down her face and along her jaw until it rested on her shoulder. "She left."

A chill swept through him, but it had nothing to do with the weather outside. "What does that mean?" He knew in his bones precisely what it meant, though he desperately wished for it to be otherwise. Any excuse would do other than the truth.

"It's my fault," Rita admitted. "You might want to sit down."

"I can't." He leaned a hand on the back of a chair, unwilling to sit but uncertain that he could continue standing. "Tell me."

Rita swallowed and turned her face toward the window. "You know, Wade, I've never done anything other than what I thought would be best for you. I wanted you to get married because I know I won't always be around. By then, you'll be an old man you'll be hard pressed to find someone who will come and take over for me. I knew you needed to find a wife, and I truly believed that Tess would be good for you. You had everything all set up for you, and I was so angry when you brought Ella here."

"I know, but that's precisely why I did it," he admitted, hearing just how childish it sounded. "You wouldn't listen to me about Tess, and I knew you'd never leave me alone until I married someone else. It wasn't the right way to do it, so we were both at fault there."

"That's generous of you." Rita sighed and smoothed her hand over the wooden surface in front of her. "I wasn't kind to her. I thought she'd leave, that she wouldn't want to stay here and put up with me just so she could marry a stranger. Surely, she had a much better life in Boston to go back to. But she was resilient, and I couldn't stand it anymore. I found her this morning, and I told her that she wasn't right for you."

His heart clenched. "You didn't."

"I did, and then I gave her every reason why. She actually had a few things to say back, though the girl certainly knows how to be polite even when the other person doesn't deserve it. She packed her bags, and she walked away."

"When was this?" Wade's fingers clamped around the back of the chair.

"A few hours ago," Rita admitted.

"She's either made it into town or she's frozen half to death by now. How could you do this?" Instead of waiting for an answer, he stormed back to the front door to get his coat.

"Because I wanted what was best for you," Rita replied stubbornly. "I might've been wrong about exactly what that was, but I tried. I really did, Wade, and I'm sorry that it's all turned out this way."

"We can discuss it when I get back." He grabbed a scarf from the rack and wound it around his neck. What had Ella been wearing when she'd left? Did she have enough to keep her warm and safe? What might've happened to her out there on the road, all alone?

Rita grabbed at his sleeve. "Please say you'll forgive me."

He loved his mother, but this was something beyond anything she'd ever done. "I guess we'll see what happens." Wade yanked open the door.

"She loves you!" Rita called behind him just before the door slammed.

He raced into town, urging his horse to go faster as the cold wind whistled in his ears as his mind whirled. Was his mother right? Did Ella truly love him? He wasn't sure he could trust anything she said now, not after this.

His heart had plenty to say on the matter, though. Wade couldn't know Ella's true feelings, but he was starting to understand his. He'd tried to tell himself that a marriage didn't have to be about love as long as it was his own choice, but the matter was far more complicated than either he or his mother had ever anticipated. It wasn't just about finding a partner, someone who could do the work and fill the role. It was about love and passion and all the blessings from God. Ella was certainly one of those blessings, and yet he'd treated her poorly.

It was Christmas Eve, and the town was nearly empty. Many of the shops had closed down while the owners went to spend time with their friends and family. It felt cold and lonely as he trotted along the main street. Wade kept his eyes open, but he knew where she must've gone. He could only hope that he wasn't too late.

He barely took the time to loop his reins through the hitching post when he reached the train station, and he hurried inside with a pit in his stomach. What was he going to do if she wasn't there?

Like the rest of town, it was nearly empty inside. The station master wasn't even at his window at the moment, and the benches were bare. Over in the corner, however, sat Ella.

She looked up, her eyes locking with his. He saw the pain in her eyes, as well as the reddened tracks down her cheeks. The hurt she suffered from stabbed straight into his own heart. He whipped off his hat and crushed it in his hands. It would take a Christmas miracle for her to forgive him. "Ella."

Chapter 11

"Wade." Ella watched him approach, once again feeling conflicted. Her heart jumped with joy every time she laid eyes upon him, yet it was quickly followed with another wave of sadness. His coming here was only going to extend her hurt.

"You're safe," he breathed as he came to stand before her. His shoulders relaxed as he let out a breath. "May I sit next to you?"

"If you'd like, though I can't imagine why you'd want to. Did Mr. Green send you?" She watched him carefully as he moved toward the bench.

He paused for a second. "Jacob? No. Why?"

"He was kind enough to give me a ride into town," she admitted. "I asked him not to tell you where I was."

Wade angled his body so that he faced her even while occupying the same bench. "But why, Ella? Why did you leave?"

She could think of nothing else but her relationship with Wade, and it was starting to wear her thin, but she might as well let it all out. "Because your mother was right."

He shook his head. "No, she wasn't," he began.

"Listen," she pleaded. "Rita told me that you needed a woman who was more adapted to this environment, who could do the work and give you everything you need. She thought I would make you unhappy. I won't say that your mother has always been right, and I surely can't agree with her methods, but there just might be something to her thought process after all."

Wade gaped at her and shook his head slightly. "I don't understand. She was terrible to you, Ella."

Ella nodded. "I don't belong out here. I thought I wanted to learn the ways of the frontier, and I thought I could become someone else by leaving my home. The truth is that I was just running away. I was engaged to a man that I didn't—couldn't— love, someone whom my parents were insisting that I marry. The only way I could think of to get out of it was to leave home and marry someone else. I'd had a lot of hope about the situation, and I never meant to do anything hurtful. I love your ranch, and this town. There are so many good things about this place, but I've been deceitful both to myself and others." She felt so ashamed of herself to admit it all out loud, but at least Wade knew.

"Oh, Ella." To her surprise, he took her hand.

"Aren't you angry with me?" she asked. She would no longer skirt around the issue at hand or wait for the appropriate time to say something. She had to know.

"No." His fingers squeezed more tightly around hers. "I can't be. You see, I wasn't honest, either."

The room swam around her, and she was glad that she was seated. "You love Tess Ingram, don't you?"

"I don't, and that's the problem precisely." Now he brought his other hand up so that he clutched hers in both of his. "My mother thought I needed a wife. Since I hadn't walked anyone down the aisle yet, she decided she would fix the problem herself. *She* wanted me to marry Tess, mostly because she's such good friends with Ida."

"Tess is a good woman," Ella admitted. "She seems so kind and sweet."

"Yes, but I don't love her. I'm quite certain that she doesn't love me, either. I thought I could bring you out here, marry you, and then the matter would be taken care of. The moment I saw you, however, I knew you deserved more than just to be carried straight to the chapel. I thought we should have some time, but then I didn't know how to handle it. I kept my distance because you were just so perfect, and I worried that I wouldn't make a good enough husband. I think I panicked a little."

Jacob had told her that he and his wife had a difficult time right at first. They'd been young and had so much to learn. Maybe she and Wade did, as well. "We were both using each other to escape the fates that awaited us otherwise."

"Yes!" He nodded emphatically. "Our motives might not have been right, but I think God has blessed us with a very fortunate accident. I never would've met you otherwise. I still want to marry you."

"Are you sure?" she dared to ask. "What if I'm not a good enough wife for you? What if my upbringing means that the two of us will be unhappy together?"

"We won't be. I don't think it matters where either of us came from. It only matters where we go from here and that we learn together. The truth is that I've fallen in love with you, Ella. I can't imagine my life without you. Will you marry me? Right now?"

She gasped. Her eyes flicked up to the clock on the wall. She still had two hours before the next train came, but Ella knew she didn't need that kind of time. She only needed Wade. He was right. They would figure it out together. "Yes, Wade. I love you, and I'll marry you."

"Come on, then." He still held her hand as he pulled her to her feet and out the door. "I think I know exactly where to find the pastor."

Ella laughed as they hurried down the street toward the church. Her dress hadn't been carefully chosen for the day, with the color and every bit of lace considered. There were no flowers to be had out here, and they certainly had no guests. It was completely unlike any wedding that she ever thought she'd have, and yet she felt as though she was floating alongside Wade as they hurried up the aisle toward Father Beck.

The ceremony was short and simple. Her cheeks burned as they thawed from the cold, but her hands were warm as she looked into Wade's eyes. The two of them had been so silly. They loved each other, and she knew now that they had right from the start. She'd fallen for him the moment she'd stepped off the train, and she wouldn't have regretted it at all if they'd gone straight to the chapel. They'd gone through a trial by fire over the last few weeks, and she knew they were coming out all the better for it. Ella vowed to herself in that moment, sending a silent promise up to God, that she and Wade would discuss whatever problems they had. If only they talked about it, everything would be all right.

"I do," she said when Father Beck asked.

The old man smiled happily and turned to Wade.

He nodded, his eyes glued to Ella. "I do. I definitely do."

After the ceremony, Wade gently kissed her on the lips. Ella blushed, smiling shyly at Wade. Her husband.

They trotted along at a brisk pace, and yet she could hardly take her eyes off her new husband. It made her so happy to be with him, to know that they no longer had to question their love.

There was just one thing that she did still have some questions about. "What will your mother say?" she asked when they could no longer see the town behind them. "She made it very obvious that she didn't approve of me as your wife."

Wade laughed. "Then I suppose she'll just have to adapt, won't she? Truthfully, Ella, I don't think you have a thing to worry about."

"I'm not so sure." She was confident in her new marriage to Wade, but she'd seen the look in Rita Monroe's eyes when she'd told Ella just what she thought of her.

He reached out and took her hand. "No matter what she thinks or says, you're my wife. That's the only thing that matters to me."

She loved that, but it didn't ease her nerves as they rode up to the house. Wade tied his horse to the porch railing before reaching up to lift Ella from the saddle. Instead of putting her on the ground, he kept her in his arms and went up the porch steps.

Ella leaned against his chest, knowing that he was the man she was meant to be with. She'd crossed thousands of miles to find him, and she'd questioned herself many times, but now she couldn't. He was right. It didn't matter what anyone else thought. This was *their* marriage.

The door slammed open and Rita came hurrying out of it, flinging her arms in the air. Her hair was a wreck, and her face was red and puffy. "There you are! Oh, you're all right! Both of you! I'm so sorry. Ella, Wade, I beg both of you to forgive me. I've been a terrible woman, and these past few hours of waiting and wondering have let me know just that. I tricked myself into thinking I was acting in your best interests, but I was only being selfish! Oh, please tell me that you'll forgive me."

Wade turned his head to look at Ella, still holding her securely in his arms. "I don't know. What do you think?"

"I truly am sorry," Rita added. "I want the two of you to get married. I can see now that you're perfect for each other, and I'll take care of every single detail of the wedding."

"There's no need," Ella replied softly as she held up her hand to display the slim band of gold the blacksmith had proudly made when Wade had shared the good news. "We've already been to the church."

"Oh, heaven! Oh, delight!" Rita pressed her hands to her face. "That's the best thing I've ever heard. Will the two of you please forgive me?"

Wade smiled at her. "Just as soon as you let me carry my wife over the threshold."

"Of course!" Rita practically jumped out of the way, and she hurried into the house after them. "It's Christmas Eve *and* the day of your wedding. The two of you deserve a wonderful supper, something truly special. Here, you sit by the fire, and I'll fix up something."

"Can I help?" Ella asked.

"No, dear." Rita reached out for her hand, and now when she looked at Ella there was only softness in her eyes. "Tomorrow. Tomorrow you can come into the kitchen with me, and I'll teach you every single thing I know. But this is your day, and I don't want you to lift a finger. Welcome to the family, darling."

Tears burned Ella's eyes as Rita headed off to the kitchen, but this time they were tears of joy.

Wade had bent down to stoke the fire, which had nearly gone out in their absence. It crackled merrily now and brought out the fresh scent of the Christmas tree. Her new husband stood and pulled her into his arms. He held her there as he looked into her eyes. "Ella, you've made me the happiest man in the world. The only thing I need for Christmas is to have you by my side. I love you, and I'm going to tell you that every day for the rest of my life."

Her heart lifted. Ella had always wanted to marry for love, but not so long ago she'd thought she'd have to give up on the notion. The world had seemed to be working against her, but the truth was that God had been guiding her in the right direction the entire time. "I love you, too. Merry Christmas, Wade."